Mrs. Rosey-Posey
and the
Empty Nest

Also titled : Mrs Rosey-Posey + The Baby Bird

Robin Jones Gunn
Illustrated by Bill Duca

"What is the price of five sparrows?
A couple of pennies? Not much more
than that. Yet God does not forget a
single one of them. And he knows the
number of hairs on your head! Never
fear, you are far more valuable to him
than a whole flock of sparrows."

Luke 12:6, 7 The Living Bible

Chariot Books™
David C. Cook Publishing Co.

Chariot Books™ is an imprint of David C. Cook Publishing Co.
David C. Cook Publishing Co., Elgin, Illinois 60120
David C. Cook Publishing Co., Weston, Ontario
Nova Distribution Ltd., Newton Abbot, England

MRS. ROSEY-POSEY AND THE EMPTY NEST
©1993 by Robin Gunn for text and Bill Duca for illustrations

Art Direction by Dawn Lauck

First Printing, 1993
Printed in Singapore
97 96 95 94 93   5 4 3 2 1

Library of Congress Cataloging-in-Publication Data
Gunn, Robin Jones
      Mrs. Rosey Posey and the empty nest/ by Robin Jones Gunn.
        p.   cm.— (An On my own book)
Summary: Mrs. Rosey Posey and the neighborhood children care for an abandoned
baby bird until it is ready to fly.
ISBN: 0-7814-0329-4
[1. Birds—Fiction. 2. Christian life—Fiction.]   I. Title
II. Series.
PZ7.G972Mqc   1993
[E]—dc20   92-12955
                                                           CIP
                                                           AC

Poppyville

Listen!

Do you hear that sound?

It sounds like a baby animal crying.

At Mrs. Rosey-Posey's house there are baby animals everywhere! There are baby kittens under the porch, baby ducks in the pond, and baby birds in the apple tree.

Rachel climbed up into the tree house to find out where the sound was coming from.

She pulled back the leaves and peeked through the branches. At first all she saw was more leaves and more branches.

Then she saw it! A bird's nest!

Rachel leaned closer and looked inside the nest.

"Where did the baby bird go?" Rachel said. "It must be near. I can hear it making a lot of noise."

Rachel looked all around for the baby bird.

"Here, baby bird! Here, baby bird!" Rachel
called. But the baby bird was not in the tree.

Rachel climbed down and looked in the soft,
green grass. Suddenly she found him!

"Hello, baby bird!" Rachel said. "Are you all
alone?"

All the baby bird said was, "Chirp! Chirp!
Chirp!"

Rachel looked and looked but didn't see any other baby birds. Very gently, Rachel picked up the baby bird and took it to Mrs. Rosey-Posey.

"Mercy me, Rachel Elizabeth!" said Mrs. Rosey-Posey. "What did you find?"

Rachel slowly lifted her hands so Mrs. Rosey-Posey could see.

"It's a baby bird," Rachel said.

"The poor little thing!" said Mrs. Rosey-Posey.
"Let's take him inside."

Rachel followed Mrs. Rosey-Posey into the
kitchen. Mrs. Rosey-Posey got a box. The box
looked like a square nest. It had feathers and
string and pieces of cloth.

Rachel gently put the baby bird into the box.
The baby bird chirped even louder than before.

Mrs. Rosey-Posey took a piece of flannel and tucked it in all around the baby bird. "He must miss his brothers and sisters. This will help keep him warm."

Then Mrs. Rosey-Posey went over to the sink and mixed up something special for the baby bird to eat.

"Rachel, would you like to feed him?"

"How?" Rachel asked.

"Like this," said Mrs. Rosey-Posey. She let three big drops fall into the baby bird's open mouth. As soon as the bird swallowed, he opened his beak and cried for more.

"He's hungry!" Rachel said.

"Baby birds are always hungry," said Mrs. Rosey-Posey. "They also like to eat bugs and worms."

"It's a good thing I found him," Rachel said, giving the baby bird another squirt of lunch. "Nobody else knew he fell to the ground."

"Oh?" said Mrs. Rosey-Posey.

Rachel looked up and Mrs. Rosey-Posey said, "There is someone else who knew."

"Did you know?" asked Rachel.

"No, not me. It was someone else."

"Who?" asked Rachel.

The baby bird closed his beak and closed his eyes.

Mrs. Rosey-Posey whispered, "He's sleepy now. Please come back tomorrow. Maybe you will be able to guess who knew when this baby bird fell to the ground."

"Is it someone who lives here?" Rachel asked.

"Yes," said Mrs. Rosey-Posey putting her hand on her heart. "It's Someone Who lives here."

The next day Rachel came back to see the
baby bird. She brought her cousin Ashley
with her. They saw Mrs. Rosey-Posey digging
in the dirt around her flowers.

"Just in time!" said Mrs. Rosey-Posey. "Our
baby bird is ready for his lunch. You can both
help me."

"He's so cute!" Ashley said when she saw the baby bird. "May I feed him? Please? May I?"

"Of course," said Mrs. Rosey-Posey. "Give him one of these." She showed Ashley the bowl full of squirmy worms.

Ashley made a very funny face. "I don't think I want to feed him anymore," she said.

Rachel laughed and said, "I will. Watch, Ashley. This is how you do it." Rachel bravely picked up a worm. The worm wiggled and wiggled. Then it wiggled right through her fingers onto the floor.

It took a long time to feed the baby bird. He ate four worms and two bugs.

"Let's have our snack on the porch," said Mrs.
Rosey-Posey. "I have something special for you."
"I hope it's not worms!" said Ashley.
"How did you guess?" said Mrs. Rosey-Posey.

On the front porch was a big box with
towels in it.

"This is your nest," said Mrs. Rosey-Posey.
"You are my baby birds. Hop in your nest and
I will give you a snack."

The girls giggled and hopped in their nest.

"Let me hear you cheep!" said Mrs. Rosey-
Posey. She wiggled a candy worm over their
heads.

Rachel and Ashley cheeped and peeped as
Mrs. Rosey-Posey fed them the candy worms.

Then Ashley said, "Mrs. Rosey-Posey, Rachel said someone lives here who knew about the baby bird. Is that true?"

"Yes," said Mrs. Rosey-Posey.

"But you are the only one who lives here," said Ashley.

"Oh? Is that so?" asked Mrs. Rosey-Posey.

"Who else lives here?" Ashley asked.

"Someone," said Mrs. Rosey-Posey.

"Who?" both girls asked.

Mrs. Rosey-Posey smiled and said, "Try to guess. It's someone who knows all about you!"

"I know! I know!" said Ashley. "It's my mom and dad!"

"Ashley!" Rachel said. "Your parents don't live here."

"Oh," said Ashley.

Mrs. Rosey-Posey leaned forward.

She spoke softly as if she was telling them a secret. "This someone even knows how many hairs you have on your head!"

The girls still could not guess who the someone was. Mrs. Rosey-Posey only smiled and said, "Please come back again and you can guess some more."

A few days later Rachel brought her cousin Lincoln with her. They found Mrs. Rosey-Posey in the kitchen. She had a frying pan with water in it.

"You're not going to cook him and eat him, are you?" asked Lincoln with his eyes open wide.

"Mercy me!" said Mrs. Rosey-Posey with a laugh. "I'm only going to give him a bath." She gently lifted the baby bird and put him in the frying pan.

The baby bird wiggled and chirped and flapped his wings. Then he shook his feathers. The water sprayed all over Rachel and Lincoln.

After his bath, the baby bird ate some worms and some berries. The children asked Mrs. Rosey-Posey for more clues.

Mrs. Rosey-Posey said, "It's the same someone who knows what you are going to say before you say it."

"I know who that is!" Lincoln said. "My grandma! She knows when I want a cookie before I even ask her."

"But Grandma didn't know that the baby bird fell from the nest," Rachel said.

"Oh," said Lincoln.

"When are you going to tell us the answer?" Rachel asked.

Mrs. Rosey-Posey looked at the baby bird.
Then she looked out the window.

"Tomorrow," she said suddenly.

"Tomorrow will be the day. Come back tomorrow. It will be a special day."

The next day Rachel, Ashley, and Lincoln
went to Mrs. Rosey-Posey's house. There were
balloons tied to the mailbox.

"A party! A party!" cried Ashley.

"Mrs. Rosey-Posey said it was a special day,"
said Lincoln. "Come on! Let's go find her!"

Before the children got to the front door, it opened.

"Welcome!" said Mrs. Rosey-Posey.

"You are just in time! Please come in!"

Mrs. Rosey-Posey had a wreath of flowers around the top of her head. Her hair stuck out the top like a big powdered-sugar donut.

"These are for you," she said to Rachel and Ashley, placing a flower wreath on their heads. "This is a very special day!"

She gave Lincoln a special hat with a big blue feather.

"Are you all ready?" Mrs. Rosey-Posey asked, picking up the baby bird and holding him in her hands.

The children nodded.

"Then follow me!" she said. They went up the stairs to the very top bedroom.

The room had a big window that opened up to a small balcony. They all climbed out the window. They had to stand closer on the balcony. They were full of excitement.

"See if you can guess now," said Mrs. Rosey-Posey. "Who is the Someone Who knew when this baby bird fell to the ground?"

The children still did not know.

"This Someone is always with you and knows everything about you," said Mrs. Rosey-Posey.

"Even how many hairs you have on your head!" said Ashley.

"Indeed!" said Mrs. Rosey-Posey. "Can you guess Who it is?"

Just then, Mrs. Rosey-Posey got that twinkle-sparkle-zing look in her eyes. She looked up into the wide blue sky and lifted up the baby bird.

Suddenly Rachel said, "I know! I know the answer! It's God! God takes care of the birds and He takes care of me!"

"Indeed!" said Mrs. Rosey-Posey. "You guessed it!"

Then with a voice as light as the wind and
as sweet as a song, Mrs. Rosey-Posey said,
"Take care of Your little one, Father God."
  She opened up her hands and the baby bird
flew away.

"Look!" Ashley cried. "Look! Look! The baby bird is flying."

They watched him flutter and swoop through the air. He landed in the cherry tree.

Lincoln put his hand into Mrs. Rosey-Posey's hand and asked, "Does God really know everything about me?"

"Oh, yes! Indeed He does," said Mrs. Rosey-Posey. "He knows everything about you and He loves you just the way you are. And so do I."

Lincoln smiled.

Mrs. Rosey-Posey looked around. "Where did the girls go?" she asked.

"I think I know," said Lincoln. "Follow me."

"Thirty-seven, Thirty-eight . . ."

Mrs. Rosey-Posey says: You never know when a baby bird might fall out of a tree in your own yard. Better have a nest ready! Find a small, strong box and fill it with bits of paper, small twigs, cotton balls, strips of cloth, and a few nice, green leaves. And remember . . . baby birds like to eat lots of worms!

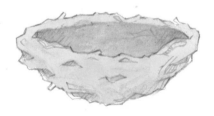